Ink Spots

Award-winning Flash Fiction & Poetry

GOLD COUNTRY WRITERS
10th Anniversary Anthology

GOLD COUNTRY WRITERS
P.O. Box 5991 Auburn CA 95604

Copyright © 2022 Gold Country Writers

Copyright for the anthology is held by Gold Country Writers, a 501(c)(3) nonprofit organization. Copyright for the individual work remains with the authors. All rights reserved. No part may be reproduced or copied without written permission of the publisher except for brief quotations in critical articles and reviews. "Olive Branch" by Georgette Unis is reprinted with express permission from Finishing Line Press.

ISBN 979-8840457863
Made in the U.S.A.
First Edition

Gold Country Writers Press

PUBLISHING TEAM
Gold Country Writers
P.O. Box 5991 Auburn, CA 95604
goldcountrywriters.com
goldcountrywriters1849@gmail.com

MANAGING EDITOR
 Chery Anderson
EDITOR
 Rebecca Inch-Partridge
PUBLISHING LIAISON
 Robin Deley
BOOK PRODUCTION
 Steve Hutchins
BUSINESS MANAGER
 Bill Baynes

GCW OFFICERS
President ~ Frank Nissen
Vice President, Internal Affairs ~ Barbara Young
Vice President, External Affairs ~ Michael O'Haver
Secretary ~ Betsy Schwarzentraub
Treasurer ~ Bill Baynes

Cover concept by Chery Anderson and Frank Nissen
Digital sketch renditions by Ernie Partridge
Ink spot images by Chery Anderson
Proofreading by Margie Yee Webb

Letter from the Editor

Gold Country Writers saved my writer's life. Between health issues, work and family obligations, I'd all but given up on becoming a published author. But the warmth and encouragement from GCW members brought my dream back to life.

This little book exemplifies GCW's mission of supporting local writers. *Ink Spots* contains work from twenty-four writers—all winners of Gold Country Writers contests. In 2016, GCW challenged members to create a story in 59 words—not one more or less—and they did. In 2017, the word count was increased to 100 words. By 2020, a poetry contest was added with a choice of themes: love or sports. The following year, the contest was changed to have a 45-line limit and no particular theme. This anthology contains all the winners of these contests.

These stories and poems are as diverse as our membership, but they were all judged by the same criteria: idea/impact and telling a good "story"; unity of effect; an engaging beginning, middle and end; mood that creates an emotion.

We hope you enjoy!

Rebecca Inch-Partridge

PRESIDENT'S NOTE

The present volume is a celebration!

Gold Country Writers has thrived for 10 years. Beginning with a modest few who shared a passion for writing, GCW has grown to provide a forum for writers in almost all genres.

Over the years, a very active schedule has evolved. The Covid-19 pandemic in 2020-2021 sorely tested our commitment and ingenuity, but our members stepped up with ideas to keep our many activities alive and well.

We are a diverse bunch with equally diverse backgrounds, bringing a lifetime's worth of experience to bear on our fellow authors' work. Our motto, "FORGING BETTER WRITERS," is not chosen lightly. This is a shirtsleeve environment where attention to the craft of writing is shared to produce the art of literature. That said, our guiding lights are goodwill and support. May these long endure.

Frank Nissen
President, July 2021-June 2023

Contents:

2016 59-WORD STORIES
Hester Jones	THE POET'S STONE	3
Pauline Nevins	A NEW LIFE	5
Margie Yee Webb	THE WALK	7

2017 100-WORD STORIES
Rebecca Inch-Partridge	WALLET	11
Nanci Lee Woody	DOWN THE DRAIN	13
Jerry Scribner	COMING HOME	17

2018 100-WORD STORIES
Chery Anderson	HOSPITAL GAMES	21
Frank Nissen	THE BARGAIN	23
Del Dozier	THE MAN IN THE ELEVATOR	25
Nanci Lee Woody	A PLAN FOR JOSH	27

2019 100-WORD STORIES
Donna Brown	MY TURN NOW	31
Chery Anderson	KINFOLK	33
Grace Bourke	A SHADOW OF DOUBT	35

2020 100-WORD STORIES
Kathleen Ward	IN WHICH HOUSING TRACTS REPLACE WOODLANDS	39
Chery Anderson	BLANK PAGE	41
Susan M. Osborn	QUEEN FOR A DAY	43
Randy Whitwell	TOMORROW	45

2020 POETRY

Cathy Cassady	SENIOR SOFTBALL	49
Indra Kapur	A HOUSE THAT I KNOW	51
Bill Baynes	ON THE WAY TO THE LAKE	55
Randy Whitwell	THE FIRE	59
Betsy Schwarzentraub	CLIMBING YOSEMITE'S WASHINGTON COLUMN	61
Karen DeFoe	BLUE-EYED QUICKSAND	63

2021 100-WORD STORIES

Bill Baynes	A FRIENDSHIP FOUND	69
Jody Brady	A SUITCASE TOO HEAVY TO CARRY	71
Rebecca Inch-Partridge	JW AT THE DOOR	73

2021 POETRY

Karen DeFoe	BLACKBERRY BUDDHAS	77
Georgette Unis	OLIVE BRANCH	81
David Anderson	WHERE HE PROPOSED TO HER	85
Indra Kapur	LITTLE KARMAS	87

2022 100-WORD STORIES

Karen Clarkson Clay	OH WHAT A LONELY BOY	93
Jerry Elmer	THE FIX	95
Rebecca Inch-Partridge	JULIE	97

2022 POETRY

Indra Kapur	DADDY'S GIRL	101
Karen DeFoe	MOURNING IN WINTER	103
Kathleen Ward	MONKEYS	105

History of Gold Country Writers	108

2016 59-Word Stories

Hester Jones

Hester Jones is a young adult fantasy writer, a poet, a quilter, and a fabric artist. She enjoys sharing family stories with Auburn Winter Storytelling Festival audiences.

First Place

THE POET'S STONE:
A CAUTIONARY TALE

Hester Jones

Two men, blinded by a moonless night, pass on a narrow path.

One is a starving vagrant, the other, a cursed victim.

Which is which?

A flashing knife rips flesh; screams dwindle into a silent death.

Flint sparks bring cursed light.

A gasp, then wails of grief as the killer leaps toward hungry boulders far below

…two dead brothers.

Pauline Nevins

Pauline Nevins is the author of two books: a memoir, *"Fudge" the Downs and Ups of a Biracial, Half-Irish British War Baby*–which includes an audio version narrated by the author–and *Bonkers for Conkers,* a collection of her newspaper columns in the *Auburn Journal* and Nevada City's *The Union*. She is currently writing her first novel.

Second Place
A NEW LIFE

Pauline Nevins

Thin fingers wet from the icy sea spray clasp the rusted rail. Wispy strands sting grey eyes narrowed against the piercing morning light. She was leaving the granite soil where seeds die. She was leaving the black-robed, the pious whose holy waters dare not flow. Her frozen hand slipped inside her grey wool coat to caress the new life.

Margie Yee Webb

Margie Yee Webb is the author and photographer of *Cat Mulan's Mindful Musings: Insight and Inspiration for a Wonderful Life*, which was awarded Certificates of Excellence for "Gift Book" and "Color Photographs" by the Cat Writers' Association. The gift book—inspired by her cat—shows Mulan's expressive, philosophical nature with humor and wisdom. Also, she is co-editor of *Not Your Mother's Book . . . On Cats*, an anthology awarded a Muse Medallion by CWA. Margie serves as Director of Speaker Programs for Gold Country Writers.

Third Place
THE WALK
Margie Yee Webb

The leaves crunching underfoot shook her from daydreaming. It had been months since their last morning walk there. Now here she is. Alone. At their park. Glancing up, she is startled by a figure ambling towards her. *Max?* She squints over her sunglasses. No. Just his doppelganger. From behind a woman croons, "Bud-dy!" Suddenly he turns, wagging his tail.

2017 100-Word Stories

Rebecca Inch-Partridge

Rebecca Inch-Partridge is a freelance editor, who specializes in speculative fiction, mysteries, and memoirs. She serves as Gold Country Writers' Director of Critique Groups and co-hosts Open Mic for the Spoken Word. Several of her short stories and articles have appeared in online and small press magazines. Her first novel, *ESCAPING THE DASHIA*, will be released in spring of 2023. www.ripartridge.com

First Place
WALLET

Rebecca Inch-Partridge

"Hey lady, give me your wallet."

"Okay. Relax. I'm not going to get myself killed over forty bucks. But I need my driver's license. I'm flying out to see my dying mother."

"I don't give a damn about your driver's license."

"Of course you don't. You must be in a bad situation to risk going to prison for armed robbery. Here's my wallet and business card. I'm a social worker."

"I'm pointing a damn gun at your head and you want to help me?"

"I believe God sent you to me for a reason."

"You can keep your damn wallet..."

Nanci Lee Woody

Nanci Lee Woody was a community college teacher and textbook author. She writes poetry, song lyrics and short stories. Her novel, *Tears and Trombones*, won the Independent Publishers Book Award for Best Regional Fiction in 2014. She recently completed the pilot episode to convert the novel for a streaming series for TV. To read samples of Nanci's work and learn about her other passion, art, go to nancileewoody.com or bookcompanion.com.

Second Place
DOWN THE DRAIN
Nanci Lee Woody

Roger. Guess what? I'm making a chocolate cake for your birthday.

Tap tap tap

I could use some help here.

Uh huh.

Are you listening to me?

Tap tap

Roger! You're like a teenager. What can be so important on Facebook right now?

Right away, Hon.

I just read that cell phones are addictive.

Tap tap

And they damage the brain.

Tap tap

Destroy relationships.

Uh huh.

CNN just reported a tornado's descending on our neighborhood.

Tap tap

Roger. Look! Your cake batter — down the drain.

Tap tap tap

OK. I'm leaving. Text me when you notice. Happy 80th.

Jerry Scribner

Jerry Scribner is a former Deputy Director of Agriculture for California and a retired attorney. He and his wife now live in Las Cruces, New Mexico. He is working on a book about California's 1981 Medfly Eradication program in Northern California. He also writes a political blog, www.democraticvotes.net.

Third Place
COMING HOME
Jerry Scribner

He came home late. The house was dark except for one lamp. She sat in the living room wearing a negligee not seen in years. Her affair had sent him away. Now she knew he had someone, too.

"You don't find me attractive, do you?" she asked.

"Of course, I do." His voice was flat.

She stood and moved toward him; eyes downcast. The loss was unbearable. He wrapped his arms around her as he kissed her tears. His face was kind. Their eyes met, then their lips.

A child's voice called, "Daddy? Are you home?"

"Yes," they answered together.

2018 100-Word Stories

Chery Anderson

Chery Anderson enjoys writing stories which pull the reader between sadness and humor. "Hospital Games" is the story of a child taking chemo, her mother trying to distract the child, and the child providing the zinger to make the reader smile. You are left with the feeling that all will work out for these two people. Chery is a past president and currently the Director of Communications for Gold Country Writers.

First Place
HOSPITAL GAMES

Chery Anderson

The nurse adjusts the IV drip, then leaves. My daughter's feverish eyes sparkle. "Want to play a game?" Smiling, I nod.

She giggles, "I'm thinking of something green."

"Pond slime from Greenland?"

"Nope."

"A green alien?"

"Nope."

"I need a clue."

"It has seeds that make you fart. Everyone in second grade knows to scrape out the dill pickle seeds."

She had given away the answer. "Hmmm. Could it be a dill pickle?"

"Yes! When I grow up, I'm going to be as smart as you!"

"Smarter." I kiss her bald head. Please God make it so, I pray silently.

Frank Nissen

Frank Nissen grew up in the heart of the Gold Country, roaming the hills and canyons through which the American River flows. He went on to work in animation for over forty years doing visual and story development for projects such as *Mulan*, *Dinosaur*, and *Tarzan*. After retiring from Disney Studios, he returned to the landscape that inspired his novel, FORTUNE'S CALL, which was released earlier this year.

Second Place (Tied)
THE BARGAIN

Frank Nissen

The foreign minister appraised his guest – a bumpkin from one of the colonies. The foreign minister listened patiently to the envoy's proposal.

"I will take your request before the emperor. Please wait." He disappeared into the next room. Inside, the emperor was supervising his war.

"It's the American, Sire," said the minister. "They want to buy Louisiana for three million dollars."

"Merde!" cried the emperor. "It's worth twice that."

"Indeed," replied the minister. "But that will buy a lot of cannons."

The emperor sighed, "Well, we may as well sell it to them. They are going to overrun it, anyway."

Del Dozier

Del Dozier is a writer, actress, and singer from Los Angeles, where she pursued a twenty-year career in theater, television, and voiceover.

Del's interest in writing began at the age of ten, when she received her first diary for Christmas. Over the years, she grew to love journal writing as a tool for self-expression. She is currently writing her memoir about overcoming childhood family dysfunction, and finding her path to healing and joy.

Second Place (Tied)
THE MAN IN THE ELEVATOR

Del Dozier

The elevator swept to a stop after the ding, a jolting reminder of my upcoming job interview with Halo.

The strikingly handsome man I'd been flirting with said, "Good luck on your interview. I'm Jeff Wagner. I hope to see you around," then gave me a wink and strode off the elevator.

Straight ahead, I saw a large Halo Group logo on the wall. As I stepped off the elevator, I realized that Halo was the only company on the floor. I walked toward the receptionist as I dug through my purse for the name of my interviewer: Jeff Wagner.

Nanci Lee Woody

In addition to writing a novel, short stories and poetry, Nanci Lee Woody is a photographer and an artist. Her work can be seen at the High Hand Gallery in Loomis. It also appears annually in the PBS/KVIE gallery and in their on-air art auction and fundraiser, in the Blue Line Arts member show, in the Rocklin Fine Arts member show, and other venues.

You can read excerpts and learn more about her award-winning novel, *Tears and Trombones*, at http://www.nancileewoody.com. You will also find there her art samples, short stories and poems.

Third Place
A PLAN FOR JOSH
Nanci Lee Woody

Mom. Dad. You're approaching 90. Shouldn't we make a plan for after you pass?

"Look at this email, Myrt."

"Our Josh is so efficient. I can't see the big hurry myself."

"We probably should talk options. Six feet under?"

"In a suffocating casket covered with dirt? I'm claustrophobic, Henry! And we wouldn't be together."

"We can't have that, Love. Let's combine our ashes, scatter them in the Pacific."

"I hate cold water. Can't swim! Sharks! Let Josh strew our ashes in the woods."

"That's illegal, Myrt."

"Let them arrest us."

"Ha! Can't wait to tell Josh we have a plan."

2019 100-Word Stories

Donna Brown

A finalist in the 2019 San Francisco Writers Conference writing contest for her novel-in-progress, *Emergency Landing*, Donna Brown holds an MA in English and an MFA in Creative Writing from San Francisco State University. Donna's short story, "Sleepwalking," was chosen for the 80th publication of *Transfer Magazine at SFSU*. The issue also featured an interview with Anne Rice and reprints of her stories from her time at SFSU.

First Place

MY TURN NOW

Donna Brown

Tipped her ladder over. She fell into those blackberry bushes she'd been pickin' at. Screamed out for me to help 'cause she didn't know I'd done it to her.

Winced a lot. Tried to get free.

On her back, ladder on top, impenetrable thicket underneath. Thorns scraping parts of her she didn't know. She managed to flip the ladder aside.

Turned herself over. Made it worse. Face and palms bleeding. She, sinking deeper, tangled in bramble, ground six feet under, sun shining.

Took me a big scoop out of her berry bucket, sweetness cooling parts of me I didn't know.

Chery Anderson

Chery Anderson grew up in New Mexico where she often listened to the "old folks" telling stories sitting on the front porch. The stories were often laced with lessons for the "young'uns" to learn. This story "Kinfolk" is about the murder of a child. The lesson is about the destruction jealousy within a family can bring. And the keeping of a family secret. Chery is the Flash Fiction Group Leader and a past president of Gold Country Writers.

Second Place
KINFOLK

Chery Anderson

Mother always hated Tuesday.

After the funeral, the police question us, the five brothers.

Sunday, the eldest, says it is God's will.

But, isn't everything?

Monday, the second eldest, suggests a lapse of common sense in the female personality.

Thursday says he knows nothing about anything. Which is his usual excuse.

And Friday, too young to guard his tongue, declares anyone can fall down the stairs.

Our brother, Saturday, the unborn baby, offers no opinion.

I, Wednesday, and I alone, understand the motive.

I stay silent because it no longer matters.

Mother always hated Tuesday but Father dearly loved her.

Grace Bourke

Grace Bourke is a writer, photographer, nature enthusiast and a quality improvement coach. She's been writing since she was a child, winning her first writing contest at the age of eleven and publishing her first magazine article while in college. She has been published in several medical journals and spoken at conferences; this is her debut publication in fiction. She is currently working on several STEAM and SEL manuscripts for children.

Her website is GraceBourke.com and she can also be found on Facebook and LinkedIn.

Third Place
A SHADOW OF DOUBT

Grace Bourke

Blackness fades to confusion. Intense pain. I'm lying in the street? The car? Smashed!

Where is he? He's trapped. Fire! It's too late. I crawl away.

I remember, now. He'd been drinking. We argued. He hit me, again.

I pressed the accelerator instead of the brake. The car sped out of control. Just before we crashed, I jumped out.

Why wasn't my seatbelt fastened?

I'm sure I yelled, "Jump!"

Why didn't he? What just happened?

As a lawyer, I know I'm innocent until proven guilty beyond reasonable doubt. It was an accident.

Wasn't it? Tears stream down my face, unchecked.

2020 100-Word Stories

Kathleen Ward

Kathleen Ward has spent over 25 years teaching writing and editing. In 2019, she received an Honorable Mention in Writer's Digest 88th Annual Writing Contest for her short story, "Barbara." She was recognized as a finalist in the 2021 San Francisco Writers Conference's competition for her novel-in-progress *Refugees in the New World – Gaby's Quest*.

First Place

IN WHICH HOUSING TRACTS REPLACE WOODLANDS

Kathleen Ward

A bit of the universe died today.

No dazzling supernova marked it, no brilliant volcano, not the tiniest seismic jolt.

Its grave was dug deep and cold with backhoes and screaming chainsaws, the tombstone set by infernally churning cement mixer.

None of us noticed the loss.

After all, there was work, school, and a jumbo sale at the mall.

We rushed by in oblivion, not even tossing a wreath from the car as we passed.

But somewhere in the soot-dusted snows of Siberia, a mother tiger nuzzled her cub and cried, and at sea, a humpback breached in silent salute.

Chery Anderson

Chery Anderson has been writing stories since she was small. A few years ago, she found oral storytelling and now writes for the spoken word. She is involved in organizing the Auburn Winter Storytelling Festival. Chery is a founding member of Gold Country Writers and a past president.

Second Place

BLANK PAGE

Chery Anderson

The writer stared at the blank page.

The blank page stared at him.

He tapped the space bar 175 spaces

from the left to the right margin.

He hit enter 30 times to the bottom of the page.

The writer stared at the blank page.

The blank page stared at him.

He centers aligns and hit caps lock for the title.

He dropped down one line and typed "by"

and his name.

He changed the font and text size.

The writer stared at the blank page.

The blank page stared at him.

Finally, he slowly typed the title: "Blank Page."

Susan M. Osborn

Susan M. Osborn, Ph.D., M.S.W., is a writer, storyteller, and editor. Her books include *The Awful Bosses Coloring Book; The System Made Me Do It! A Life Changing Approach to Office Politics*; and *Assertive Training for Women*. Currently she is working on a new book, *Looking at the World with New Eyes: A Systems Perspective*.

Third Place
QUEEN FOR A DAY
Susan M. Osborn

I was the tallest kid in first grade and had the biggest feet. Feeling fat, I hated changing clothes for gym in front of the other girls.

Anguish about my appearance was rekindled when I enrolled at the University of Colorado. Popular girls were wealthy and beautiful like Marilyn Van Derbur who became Miss America. The closest I came to being royalty was to share the same last name as a homecoming queen.

Years later, at a class reunion, several male classmates saw my name tag and greeted me enthusiastically. (They mistook me for her. I didn't correct their mistake.)

Randy Whitwell

Randy Whitwell has been interested in writing short stories and poetry since his pre-teen years. His writing tends to be fairly eclectic. He loves changing up his style, using humor, sorrow, sometimes outrage, and, often using cryptic language to present his message. His articles have appeared in the *Auburn Journal*.

He believes words are sacred and tries to follow the advice he once read from an unknown author, "If you want someone to be interested in what you say…say something interesting."

Honorable Mention
TOMORROW

Randy Whitwell

Shedding any pretense I may have formerly exhibited, I promptly removed the embroidered linen banyan mother had so lovingly fashioned for me before her untimely passing.

I then donned the finely tailored tweed trousers and coarse woolen shirt that father always said more befitted a man of "substance and character."

I can never be that man, never in his eyes.

Weakness is the only cloak I shall ever wear.

Yet mother loved me. She once said, "No man need stand in the shadows for light will follow those who choose the sun."

That light eludes me still. But perhaps tomorrow...

2020 Poetry

Cathy Cassady

Cathy Cassady is the daughter of Neal and Carolyn Cassady. She has published two books based on her mother's writing, *Travel Tips for the Timid* and *Poetic Portrait*. Cathy presents a PowerPoint program detailing the lives and literary contributions of her parents. In 2019, she traveled to several destinations in the East for a month-long speaking and book-signing tour. Look for Cathy's upcoming graphic biography based on her father's traumatic childhood: *Young Neal Cassady*. www.cathycassady.org

First Place in "Sports" Category

SENIOR SOFTBALL:
From a Fan's Point of View

Cathy Cassady

Batters comin', batters goin'
Runnin', catchin', slidin' by.

Lights are hummin', fans are screamin',
"What's the score? Don't hit a fly!"

Blue keeps watchin', balls keep zoomin'
Hits and fouls and outs abound.

Though the players try to catch 'em
Some flies end up on the ground.

From the dugout player's whistlin'
Coaches yellin', "Hustle! Run!"

Though it seems like they're disgusted,
In the end, it's all for fun.

This is just the perfect hobby,
Smilin', laughin', jokin' all.

Nothin' beats the rush that's given
Those who play SENIOR SOFTBALL!

Indra Kapur

Indra Kapur likes the brevity and punch of short stories and poems. Her story, "To The Letter" won honorable mention in Writer's Digest 78th Short Story Contest and, "The Seventh Chair" won honorable mention in Writer's Digest 79th Short Story Contest. She edited speeches and articles for many years before writing fiction and non-fiction pieces set in India and the west. Her short story collection, *In Any Given Room*, will be published in 2022.

First Place in "Love" Category
A HOUSE THAT I KNOW

Indra Kapur

On a street that I know
There's a two-story house
With a pool and a swing
To the sky

A creek runs below
Where the deer come
To feed and the fairies
Dance on the dew

Two little girls reside
In this house, with a K
And a C in their names

When summer arrives
They swim in the pool,
And if magic was magic,
They'd dance on the dew
By the house with
A swing to the sky

Angels sit on the roof,
Keeping all that's below
Safe in their reverent hands

Sam loves her girls,
Oh, just times a
Billion grains of sand

Love fills the rooms
Of this house that I know
So much that it holds off the rain

A great love arrives by a road
Through the woods and he
Helps to lessen the strain

His love surrounds the
Girls and their mom, it's
Magic you all aught to
Know, for however hard
Life sends down the rain,
It simply makes all
Their love grow.

Bill Baynes

Bill Baynes is a writer – producer – director, who has worked in many different media formats, ranging from newspapers and television to feature films, magazines and websites. He has three books— *Bunt*, a young adult baseball novel; *The Occupation of Joe*, a historical fiction in Tokyo, 1945; and *The Coyote Who Braved Baseball*, a middle-grade novel —released by three different indie publishers. He has placed short stories and poetry in various literary magazines.

Second Place in "Sports" Category
ON THE WAY TO THE LAKE
Bill Baynes

on the way to the lake
near dawn Saturday
stopped at Saratoga
fog thick and chill
the smell of mown grass
turned earth
            dampness

a whicker a chuff
a slap of leather
a measured exertion
coming louder closer
still invisible
a running rhythmic
            music

in full harness a horse
bursts from the mist
the big wheels
the seated man
little mouth clicks
churn past us
        disappear

into the muted light
and the men at the rail
chuckle in the quiet
soft whistles of respect
and one leans over
and slaps my back
        "Magic!"

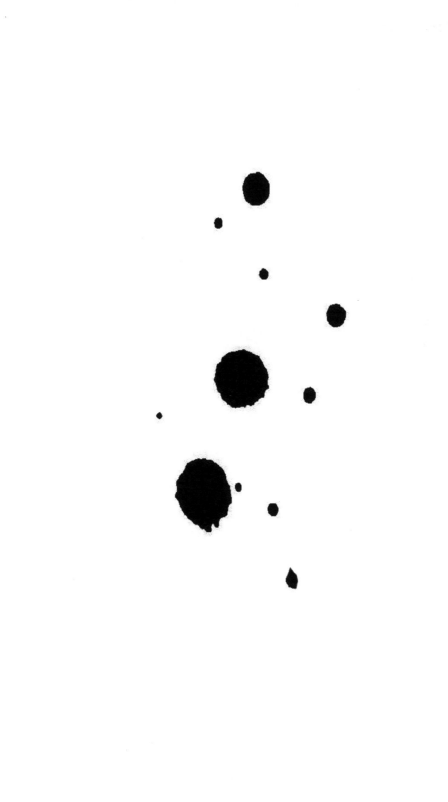

Randy Whitwell

Randy Whitwell has been interested in writing short stories and poetry since his pre-teen years. His writing tends to be fairly eclectic. He loves changing up his style, using humor, sorrow, sometimes outrage, and, often using cryptic language to present his message. His articles have appeared in the *Auburn Journal*.

He believes words are sacred and tries to follow the advice he once read from an unknown author, "If you want someone to be interested in what you say…say something interesting."

Second Place in "Love" Category
THE FIRE

Randy Whitwell

Mother goddess

faceless she waited

An old walking stick she was

Her ancient bones

Warmed by the fire

Looking for her lover

In the smoke and flames

Indian blue blanket

Wrapped around her shoulders

She remembers those times

The warm touch of his hands

The laughter

They touched the sky those two

and she remembers...

The day his feather drifted from the clouds

To rest in her heart forever

She draws the blanket close

And she is warmed by the fire

Betsy Schwarzentraub

Betsy Schwarzentraub's newest book, *Tossed In Time: Steering by the Christian Seasons*, helps readers follow the Christian worship seasons at home, find a weekly anchor, and observe daily hours reflecting dimensions of faithful living.

A national consultant and retired minister, Betsy is also author of three books on stewardship: *Growing Generous Souls: Becoming Grace-Filled Stewards*, *Afire With God*, and *Stewardship: Nurturing Generous Living*. For blogs, studies, and more, see www.generousstewards.com.

Third Place in "Sports" Category
CLIMBING YOSEMITE'S WASHINGTON COLUMN
Betsy Schwarzentraub

Her eyes this close to the granite face
see its immensity down to each inch:
feldspar, mica and quartz, enough to cinch?

Experienced fingers dusted with chalk
search for a flake to bodily jam,
or solid crack to wedge with a cam.

The heights she once held in her mind's eye
come down to each hold in the cold dawn —
the thrill of the real, ideal images gone.

Karen DeFoe

Karen DeFoe - actress, director, choreographer, celebrated teacher and poet—earned a BA in Drama and an MA in Education, served as Director of Drama for Carmichael School of Performing Arts, founded children's theater company Corps de Jeune, and performed with San Jose Music Theater, Roadside Theater in Germany, and Bacchus Playhouse in Sacramento. She taught English and Drama for 35 years and currently writes poetry for catharsis and celebration.

Third Place in "Love" Category
BLUE-EYED QUICKSAND

Karen DeFoe

I watch the amber liquid
spill over the crackling ice.
One sip softens the thickness of
my constricted throat
but cannot calm the dull ache
of my buckled heart.

I never thought
I'd reach this lonely place in time
where flashbacks disrupt
the quiet stillness and
my tangled thoughts of you
in Wrangler jeans   a Pendleton shirt
the scent of Jade East cologne
those enchanting azure blue eyes
that haunt me still.

I remember the pungent smell of manzanita
endless stars on a summer night
the bitter-sweet taste of champagne cocktails
the music of Billy Joel's *Piano Man*
soft whispers pulling me in
the comfort of your seasoned touch
no longer mine.

I never dreamed of
losing first place
second place
in the race to be in—to be with—
to be.

I never imagined
the slamming of the door—

solitary evenings   a table for one
a silenced voice
endless weekends   sleepless nights
the encounter with
"Nothing".

I never realized how fast
things change
love fades
life turns
in different directions
going nowhere   as
memories linger
like clinging cobwebs
I can't brush away.

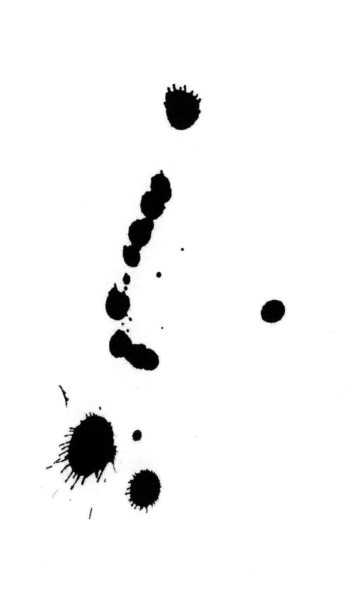

2021 100-Word Stories

Bill Baynes

Bill Baynes is a writer – producer – director, who has worked in many different media formats, ranging from newspapers and television to feature films, magazines and websites. He has three books— *Bunt*, a young adult baseball novel; *The Occupation of Joe*, a historical fiction in Tokyo, 1945; and *The Coyote Who Braved Baseball*, a middle-grade novel —released by three different indie publishers. He has placed short stories and poetry in various literary magazines.

First Place
A FRIENDSHIP FOUND

Bill Baynes

They come toward me, the Boss, as usual, in the lead. He runs with wings wide, discarding all goosely dignity, his neck normally bent backward like a horn stretched straight.

Horribly honking: "Gimme! Gimme!"

I hear a scream—a little girl between me and the onrushing flock. I swoop her up, deposit her on a large rock, out of reach.

"What an awful noise!" She scowls.

I hand her a crust. "Throw it to him."

She does and laughs as Boss stuffs his mouth, then tosses back his neck to swallow.

"I'm Anna," she says.

"I'm the Bread Man."

Jody Brady

Jody Brady, a native of Kansas City, MO, graduated with a BA in Sociology and Psychology and graduate work in Physical Education. She raised two sons while owning Jody's Sweat Shops in Colorado, and Good Stuff Coupons in Walnut Creek, CA. Her love of travel inspired her series of travel books for her five grandchildren. Her latest is *Learning about Yosemite with Grandma*. www.jodywrites.com

Second Place

A SUITCASE TOO HEAVY TO CARRY

Jody Brady

Ralph was sweating and struggling, dragging a huge bag down the street.

Harvey asked him, "What is that?"

"It's a suitcase too heavy to carry," Ralph said.

"The cage of a canary?" asked Harvey.

"No, a suitcase too heavy to carry."

"A painting of Typhoid Mary?"

"No, a suitcase too heavy to carry."

"A swimsuit made of terry?"

"No! A suitcase too heavy to carry."

"A rock found on the prairie?"

"No! A suitcase too heavy to carry."

"A pie that tastes like cherry?"

"No! Are you a religious man?"

"No," Harvey said.

"Good," Ralph said and shot him.

Rebecca Inch-Partridge

Rebecca Inch-Partridge started telling stories when she was five years old. She wrote her first novel featuring her fictitious universe, The Paraxous Star Cluster, in 8th grade. That story served as the inspiration for her young adult science fiction novel, *ESCAPING THE DASHIA*, coming out spring of 2023 by Black Rose Writing. For a sneak peek and to listen to her audio stories go to: www.ripartridge.com

Third Place
JW AT THE DOOR
Rebecca Inch-Partridge

I stood at the door next to my mother, eager to share the latest issues of the AWAKE! Magazines.

As a know-it-all teen, I felt ready to overcome any objections the householder might try. But I certainly wasn't ready for the man to come to the door naked.

I froze. Mom's hand shot out to cover my eyes.

"We won't keep you," she told the man calmly. "You must be freezing."

It was 80 degrees that day. The man sputtered and closed the door.

Years later, I got her joke and realized my Bible thumping mother was pretty darn cool.

Karen DeFoe

"Poetry is the music that helps me know and understand who I am—where I have been—where I have yet to go. It is the calm at the epicenter of chaos—the voice of reason amidst the clamor of dissidence and insanity. Writing poetry has taught me careful observation and attention to detail."

First Place
BLACKBERRY BUDDHAS
Karen DeFoe

Last night   I dreamed of summer
a kaleidoscope of images moving in dream time—

familiar country roads   fields of alfalfa
the sun setting behind endless rows of cotton
Grandpa's tractor   Grandma's gladiolas
the old grey Desoto   the wringer washing machine
the tire swing hanging from the walnut tree
mud pies in aluminum tins baking in the August sun
on the cracked sidewalk

of us—
running   laughing
picking berries from tangled vines by the dry creek bed.

Blackberries sagged on the vines—
fat little buddhas
sweetness oozing from their thicket   and we
sticky to our elbows   hands full
filled our mouths   our tin buckets   and
danced on sunburned feet   down the dirt road.

Shaded by the canopy of the walnut tree
we blew the fuzz from dandelions   watched it
float away in the summer breeze.
You kissed my cheek— your mouth   soft   round.
I placed a crown of daisies on your head.

We shimmied up the apricot tree   picked its honeyed delights
sucked pulp from plums the size of tennis balls
ate watermelon on the back porch—
our legs dangling over the cement steps—
juice running down our arms   attracting
a line of little black ants.

We itched from turning somersaults in the grass
made wishes on white butterflies
captured blue-bellied lizards   kept them
in shoe boxes with tiny holes
poked through the lids.

At nightfall—
moonlight streaming through
open windows—
we listened to   a chorus of
crickets   cicadas   owls   bullfrogs—
their music lulling us to sleep.

This morning—
I smiled   as I picked a daisy from
a supermarket bouquet—
slipped it in my pocket—   and
went to buy blackberries.

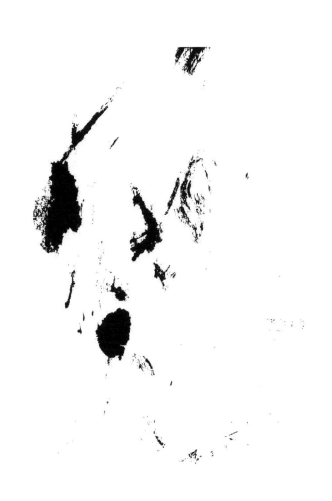

Georgette Unis

Georgette Unis is the author of two books of poetry, *Tremors* (2018) and *Watercolors in the Desk Drawer* (2022) which contains this poem published by Finishing Line Press. She leads the Gold Country Writers poetry workshop and is a member of the Ravens poetry group. In addition to her work as a poet, she has an MFA in mixed media painting.

Second Place
OLIVE BRANCH
Georgette Unis

A dove flies into
my studio window,
with tail and wings
fanned in flight,
sunlight on the tips
of its feathers
in a symphony
of whites, soft grays
and memories
of its singular melody.

When doves coo
in the morning,
I become a child
awakening to avian sounds
as they warm themselves
over telephone lines
against a brilliant sky,
musicians and
easy targets.

In the garage,
my mother's back to me,
her pale green dress
tied with a gingham apron,
she labors removing feathers
from my brother's cache.
I ask why

he killed the doves.
She complains
of so much effort
for barely a morsel,
terminates his escapades
after a wayward bone
pierces her hand.
To my young mind,
these are Noah's doves,
one, a divine messenger
to the weary ark of pairs.

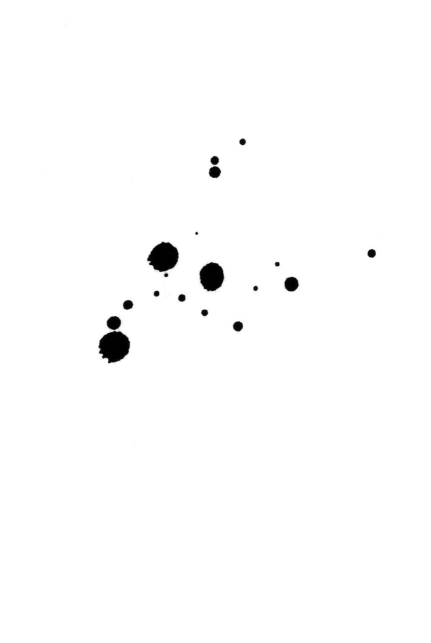

David Anderson

David Anderson was raised on Rocky Dell Orchard, near Newcastle in Placer County's Loomis Basin. After retiring from the UC Davis Library, he returned to the muse who introduced herself when he was in high school. Some of his poems have appeared in *Brevities, California Quarterly, Epiphany, Song of the San Joaquin*, and *Time of Singing*. He complains that the muse mumbles and he doesn't hear well enough to catch it the first time she speaks, so he revises and revises.

Third Place (Tied)
WHERE HE PROPOSED TO HER
David Anderson

When my mother died
I had no more words—
I had spent my grief
    in her last days
as her mind drained—
an empty sieve,
a stone worn smooth.

I could only
think of the day
my father asked me
to drive him
to Lake Tahoe
    where we stood
and gazed
at the transparent blues
of water and sky.

Indra Kapur

"I've always loved India and especially the beautiful street children of Punjab. Some live their whole lives in train stations. Their adaptability and sense of kismet are both amazing and heartbreaking. They inspire me to be a better person."

Third Place (Tied)
LITTLE KARMAS

Indra Kapur

The boy, about eight, tugs on my coat
I'm hungry, his sad eyes do say
I dig in my purse, two rupees I find
kept ready for just such a day

His sister runs up, her eyes full of hope
Thank Ram, at last we can eat
I dig a bit more and bring up some coins
Maybe now they can have a real treat

The night train arrives from Calcutta,
But the boy and the girl do not leave
They rock to and fro on bare little feet
Their clothes tissue thin, not even a sleeve

People rush up the stairs bent on their tasks,
A beggar means nothing you see,
For karma takes care of the hungry
The ship in this vast human sea

The boy and the girl in their previous lives
Earned this fate as everyone knows,
How foolish are we who give money
When hunger is what their fates chose

I look once again and my heart does a turn
For there, leaning up on the wall,
The girl is now holding an infant,
New-born and wrapped in a shawl

She's bought some milk from a vendor
And soaked her blouse in the cup,
But the baby's too weak to suckle
And the girl must finally give up.

Ours eyes meet again for a moment,
She is old beyond her young years,
Then she raises her hand and bids me farewell,
as we retreat in defeat to our tears.

2022 100-Word Stories

Karen Clarkson Clay

Karen Clarkson Clay is a memoirist, poet, investigative journalist and nonfiction writer. Her current project, *Starry Night Sketches: Oakland-Berkeley-San Quentin-Carmel - A Quirky Impressionist Memoir*, includes thirty-three short stories, from adolescent antics to oddball jobs, some lasting a single day—mortuary to massage parlor. Provocative stunts pepper the author's life. She's a magnet for mayhem and mischief as she collides with kismet.

First Place
OH WHAT A LONELY BOY

Karen Clarkson Clay

Bart tiptoed into his mother's closet. The eleven-year old grabbed a handful of hanging clothes and shook them, whipping up her fragrance. He inhaled. A tear escaped, but he wiped it quickly away.

"Big boys don't cry," Dad had said on that cold summer morning.

Bart had shivered then, and all day, through the service, in the graveyard.

The calico dress slipped off the hanger. He struggled with the zipper in the back.

At the full-length mirror he closed his eyes.

"Please can I see you?"

Instead of a Heavenly vision, his father's reflection stood beside him. Bart's knees buckled.

Jerry Elmer

Jerry Elmer is a retired electronics engineer, writer, poet, photographer and general wiseacre. He lives in the Sierra Nevada Foothills and enjoys throwing snowballs in the summer.

Second Place
THE FIX

Jerry Elmer

My craving is almost overwhelming. Dry mouth, pounding heart, knotted stomach —I know the symptoms. The acrid smell of garbage rips my nostril as I race down the alleyway, a shortcut to my source. A sharp pain racks my leg as I bark my knee running past a dumpster. The wound stings as my jeans rub on the bloody scrape. Ignore pain, concentrate on the goal: get there before it's too late!
Sprint through the park, tear around the corner. Whew, I made it! Bruno's waiting to sell me my fix.
Still five minutes till closing at Kelly's Doughnut Shop.

Rebecca Inch-Partridge

Besides being an author and freelance editor, Rebecca Inch-Partridge is a writing instructor. She teaches a "Write that Book in 9 Weeks" workshop, where students learn how to get that first draft out of their heads and onto the page. She also is a professional storyteller and does guest lectures. She loves collaborating with other authors and is currently co-authoring two cozy mystery novels. Her young adult science fiction novel, *ESCAPING THE DASHIA*, comes out in spring 2023.

Third Place
JULIE
Rebecca Inch-Partridge

Julie exits the rest stop bathroom to find his truck gone. He's done this before. He'll come back when he thinks she's learned her lesson. She cries as she tries to figure out what to do. Her sister lives three hours away. He'll be back by then and there will be no escape.

A highway patrol car sits at the end of the parking lot. She gathers her nerves and approaches the officer.

He looks out the window at her. His expression is hard; tone unwelcoming. "Can I help you, ma'am?"

"No. Never mind. My husband will be here soon."

Indra Kapur

"There are so many stories around us waiting to be heard and told. Each line, each paragraph can hold an entire life, or just a moment that changes that life forever. Never underestimate the poem or the short story. There's a lot to be said for brevity."

First Place
DADDY'S GIRL

Indra Kapur

Your bright smile, dimpled chin
Eyes a warm gold brown,
Oh yes, my sweet, you're Daddy's
Girl, his princess with a crown

Hold his picture close my love
Sit quietly with me,
We'll sing his favorite hymns today
We'll make him proud, you'll see

The guns are pointed to the sky
An honor few receive, now remember him
With arms held wide, oh, you're too
Young to grieve

Everyone's so caring, people
Are too kind, hands are reaching out
To us but I've gone somehow blind

Daddy rests beneath the stone
In perfect rank and file,
Now take the flag and thank the man,
You don't need to smile.

Karen DeFoe

"I find great inspiration in the poetry of the Romantics - in their belief that poetry is about the human experience and their lyricism which speaks to the language of the heart. I write poetry to engage the senses —to explore the human condition—to celebrate the inherent peace and joy found in nature and all things beautiful."

Second Place
MOURNING IN WINTER
A Hybrid Sonnet for Francesco and Will

Karen DeFoe

The frigid hand of winter has begun
To paint the sky in steely shades of gray
And dim the light and warmth of Autumn's sun
To lengthen hours of darkness in the day.
While Boreas exhales his icy breath
And bends the boughs that shake against the cold,
The frost from naughty Jack brings sudden death
To comely flowers I could once behold.
A melancholy madness may portend
The rolling fog—the sleet—the freezing snow,
But I, with April heart, do not intend
To dwell on winter's darkness or its woe.
    For frost will thaw and bluebirds soon will sing,
    As light returns and new life blooms in spring.

Kathleen Ward

Kathleen Ward has spent over 25 years teaching writing and editing. In 2019, she received an Honorable Mention in Writer's Digest 88th Annual Writing Contest for her short story, "Barbara." She was recognized as a finalist in the 2021 San Francisco Writers Conference's competition for her novel-in-progress *Refugees in the New World – Gaby's Quest*.

Third Place
MONKEYS
Kathleen Ward

Greg believes
that every tree
holds monkeys
in its branches.
Each tree we pass
on our daily walk
must be inspected
carefully, lovingly,
for primate habitation.
Chattering leaves
and rustling boughs
fire his small-boy heart,
and he keeps looking—
a leaping, jabbering
simian child
searching for his soul-mates.

At two, Greg doesn't understand
about cages and bars
and curious stares;
he runs free and imagines
his chimps do too.

I know
there are no monkeys wild
in Northern California,
but Greg believes,
so I look with him,
humoring him, and praying
we'll find one.

History of
GOLD COUNTRY WRITERS
Forging Better Writers

When asked about the secret to being a famous author, Ernest Hemingway once said, "There's nothing to writing. All you do is sit down at a typewriter and bleed."

Anyone who has tried to write a story knows the truth of his words. The solution is to take a break from the blood-letting to meet others with the same secret obsession. They can commiserate about your muddled plot, the sad characters, or blank pages staring at you every day. This desire to share and be inspired is the reason Gold Country Writers was first organized in Auburn, California.

In 2010, a local bookstore owner invited several customers who were both readers and writers to drop by a local coffee shop to chat. After a year, this group had outgrown the coffee shop and moved to the back room of another local morning hangout.

Along the way the group welcomed speakers to share their expertise, partnered with the Friends of Auburn Library for a day-long book festival, and set up an Indiegogo crowdfunding project. GCW members had a common goal: to encourage each other to become better writers.

The group affiliated with the Arts Council of Placer County in 2012. Meetings moved to the Arts Council building for the next three years. Again, membership growth prompted GCW to move to a new home in the Bethlehem Lutheran Church in 2015. That was the year GCW became a 501(c)(3) nonprofit organization.

Ink Spots

Since 2019, Gold Country Writers has been meeting in the large Rose Room of Auburn City Hall every Wednesday morning. The organization continues to present monthly speaker programs open to the public. Drop-in Critique meetings give members a chance to read from their work and receive feedback. Several spin-off critique groups meet in homes and restaurants with other writers working in the same genre.

The GCW Mentor Program matches members to work one-on-one to accomplish specific writing goals. All members are encouraged to attend Read & Review where our authors' published books are read, discussed and reviewed. GCW sponsors an Open Mic for the Spoken Word event at the local library where storytellers and writers gather to share their work. In months with a fifth Wednesday, the organization schedules special events. It has become a fun social event with networking as the basis.

Twice a year, GCW sponsors writing contests for members. Both the 100-word story and the poetry contests are popular. This book is a compilation of the award-winning entries.

From an ad hoc group discussing books in a coffee shop to the present organization, it's been a journey of writers looking for blank paper to apply their ink spots.